PIGS
from 1 to 10

ARTHUR GEISERT

Houghton Mifflin Company
Boston

For Bonnie

Walter Lorraine 〰 Books

Copyright © 1992 by Arthur Geisert

www.houghtonmifflinbooks.com

Library of Congress Cataloging-in-Publication Data

Geisert, Arthur.
    Pigs from 1 to 10 / Arthur Geisert.
        p. cm.
    Summary: Ten pigs go on an adventurous quest. The reader is asked
to find all ten of them, and the numerals from zero to nine, in each
picture.
    CL ISBN 0-395-58519-8   PA ISBN 0-618-21611-1
    [1. Pigs – Fiction. 2. Picture puzzles. 3. Counting.] I. Title.
II. Title: Pigs from one to ten.
PZ7.G2724Pf 1992
[E] – dc20   92-5097
                                                                        CIP
                                                                        AC

Printed in Singapore
TWP 10 9 8 7 6 5

PIGS *from* 1 *to* 10

One night, Mother read us a book about a
lost place with huge stone configurations. We
thought we knew where the place was; and we
were determined to find it.

*Throughout the quest, there are ten pigs and the
numerals 0, 1, 2, 3, 4, 5, 6, 7, 8, and 9 hiding in
each picture.*

Early the next morning, we went to the bottom of the hill, where the cannon

was stored. We started to drag it up the road.

We pulled and we pushed.

We aimed the cannon carefully. We filled it with black powder, put a grappling

hook into the barrel, and then lit the fuse.

BOOM!

The hook shot out!

The hook caught, and the rope stretched taut behind it. Grasping the rope,

we started across the abyss.

Balancing carefully, we built a bridge.

With picks and pry bars we dug into the rock.

The rock was harder than we thought.

We had to get a large steam drill.

Finally we drilled through the rock.

There it was!

We had found the place that Mother read about.

We brought over a saw and carefully copied each stone configuration.

We headed home in triumph.

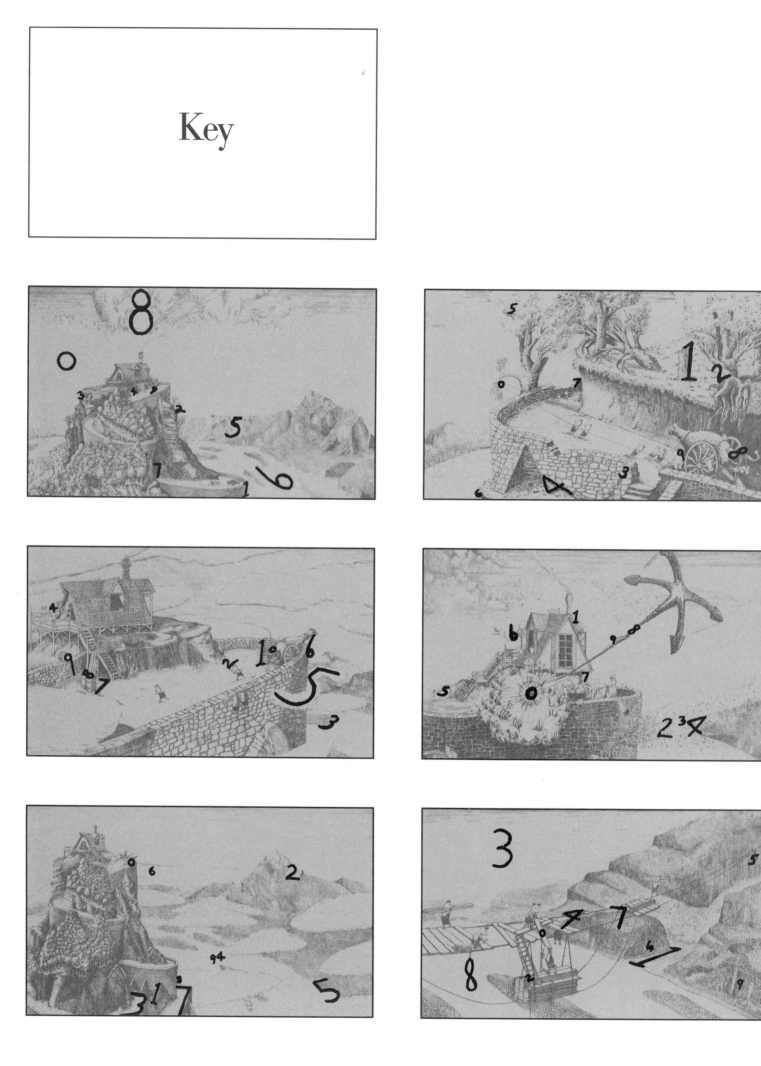

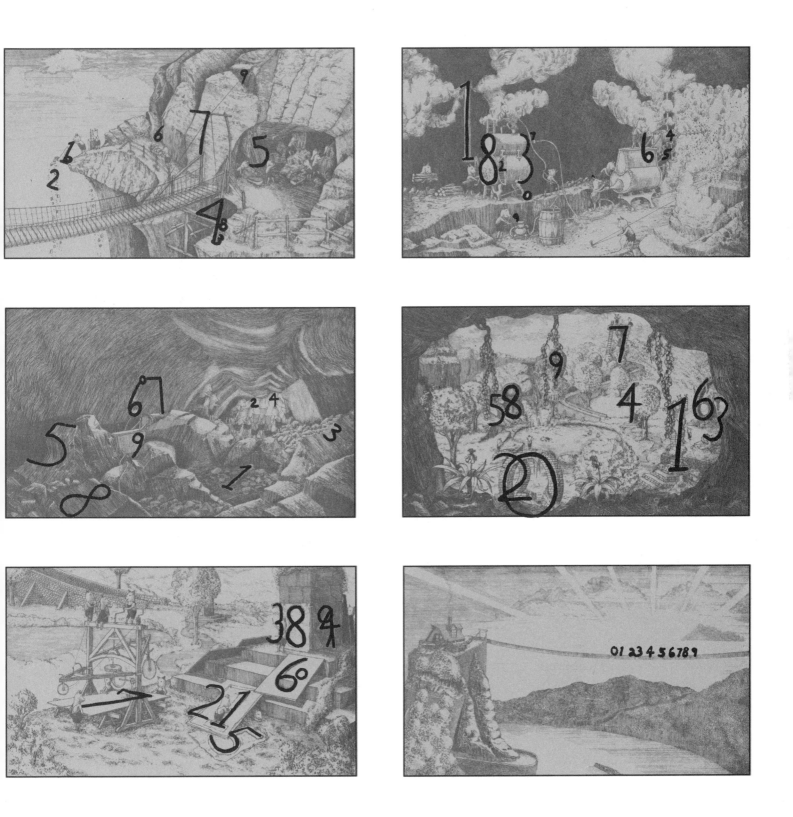